To Jenn,

The last time I saw
you hold Nadia I was just
awestruck at the love you showed
toward that precious baby, it was
an emotion I could actually feel
I am thrilled you
are part of my
life "God Bless
you always)
"Mom Carol"
2006

2⁰⁰

To Ericka, whose journey into motherhood inspired this book.
To Mar, my soulmate, who will live it.
And to my parents, who fulfilled all their promises to me.

 లు Lisa Humphrey ಲ

 లుౄ

For my mother and father, Evelyn and Don—
their love taught me to love.
And for my children, Carissa and Jaron,
their mother, Patricia, and our families.
All of you are within these pages.

A grateful thanks to Holly and Kris Hamper and
their daughters, Keilana and Jinaya;
and to Chie and Bruce Sharp and
their triplets, Erika, Kai and Lena.

 లు David Danioth ಲ

A Mother's Promise

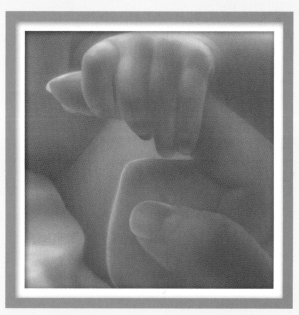

Written by Lisa Humphrey

Illustrated by David Danioth

ILLUMINATION
Arts

Publishing Company, Inc.

Bellevue, Washington

A Terri Cohlene Book

When you are born...

I promise to help you remember
all you have forgotten.

I promise the ocean...

you will hear the beating of its heart
against the shores.

I promise the forests...

you will share the whispers
of their pines.

I promise the desert...

you will feel its warm breath
on your cheek.

I promise the mountains...

*you will sit on their broad shoulders
and wonder.*

I promise the stars...

you will follow their pathways
and hear their stories.

I promise the world's sacred places...

I will teach you honor.

I promise the world's creatures...

I will teach you respect.

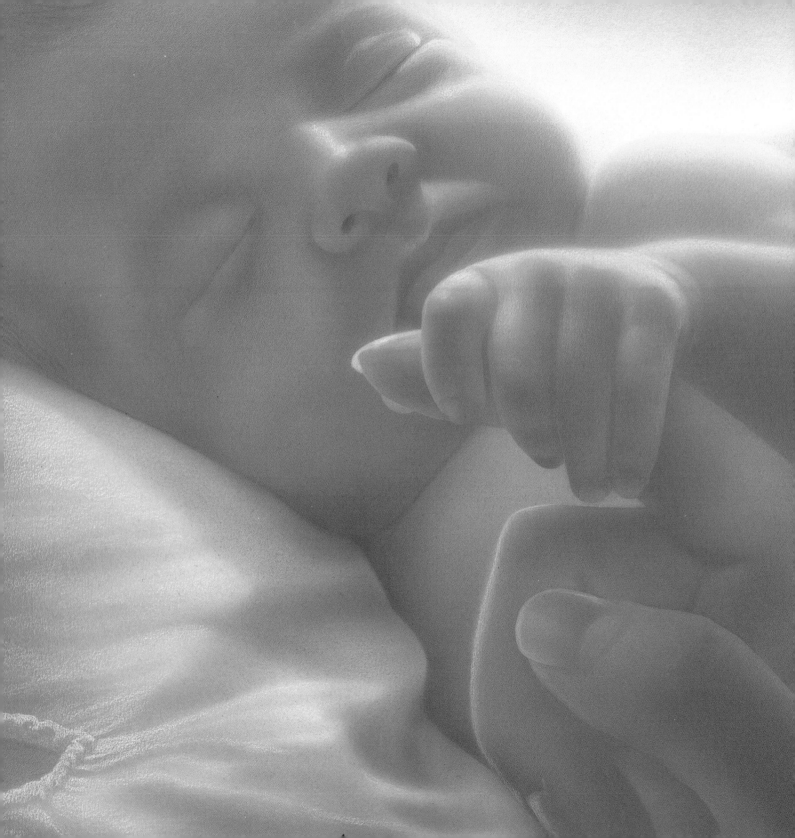

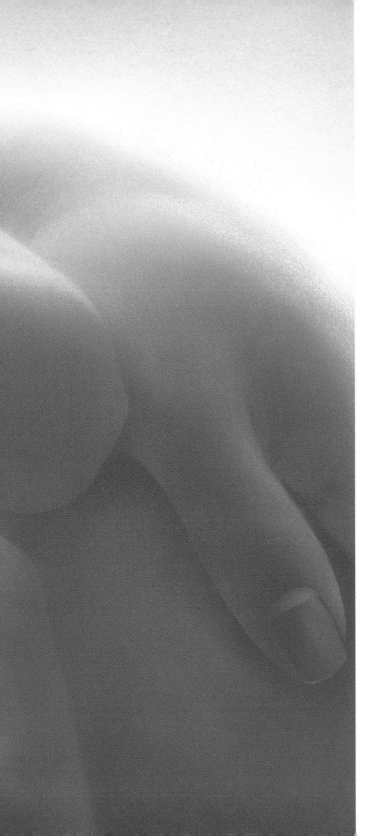

I promise the world's people...

I will teach you to love—
just as I promise to always love you.

And the Universe will answer,

creating you
from the white sands of Egypt,
the emerald moss
of the ancient forests,
the blue salt of the Pacific,

While the winds lace you together with silvery moonlight.

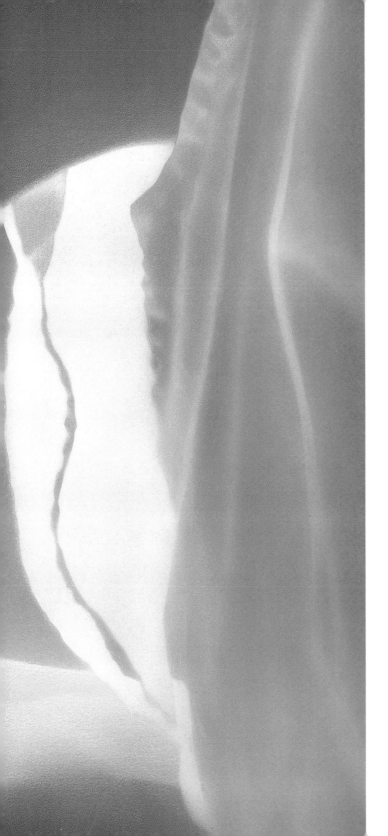

And when you arrive,
you will recognize me.
We will celebrate the joy
of our togetherness.

Beneath the light of your first dawn,
the sun will wash you in gold

And welcome you again
as you remember your promise
to the world.

Publishing Company, Inc.

P.O. Box 1865 ∽∽∽ Bellevue, WA 98009

Tel: 425-644-7185 ∽∽∽ 888-210-8216 (orders only) ∽∽∽ Fax: 425-644-9274

liteinfo@illumin.com ∽∽∽ www.illumin.com

Library of Congress Cataloging-in-Publication Data

Humphrey, Lisa, 1970-
   A mother's promise / by Lisa Humphrey ; illustrated by David Danioth.
     p. cm.
   Summary: A mother promises her unborn child the ways in which they will celebrate their
relationship and love, honor, and respect the world around them.
   ISBN 0-9701907-9-4
   [1. Mother and child--Fiction.] I. Danioth, David, 1956- ill. II. Title.

PZ7.H8965Mo 2004
[Fic]--dc22
                                                                                          2003062078

Published in the United States of America

Printed in Singapore by Tien Wah Press
Book designer: Molly Murrah, Murrah & Company, Kirkland, WA

Illumination Arts is a member of Publishers in Partnership—replanting our nation's forests.